Withdrawn

TECH PIONEERS™

ADA LOVELACE

GINA HAGLER

ROSEN PUBLISHING
NEW YORK

Published in 2016 by The Rosen Publishing Group, Inc.
29 East 21st Street, New York, NY 10010

Copyright © 2016 by The Rosen Publishing Group, Inc.

First Edition

All rights reserved. No part of this book may be reproduced in any form without permission in writing from the publisher, except by a reviewer.

Library of Congress Cataloging-in-Publication Data

Hagler, Gina.
 Ada Lovelace / Gina Hagler. — First Edition.
     pages cm. — (Tech pioneers)
 Includes bibliographical references and index.
 ISBN 978-1-4994-6282-1 (library bound)
 1. Lovelace, Ada King, Countess of, 1815–1852—Juvenile literature. 2. Women mathematicians—Great Britain—Biography—Juvenile literature. 3. Mathematicians—Great Britain—Biography—Juvenile literature. 4. Computers—History—19th century. 5. Calculators—History—19th century. I. Title.
 QA29.L72H34 2015
 510.92—dc23
 [B]
                        2015022070

Manufactured in the United States of America.

Contents

INTRODUCTION 4

Chapter One
ENGLAND IN THE TIME OF ADA LOVELACE 8

Chapter Two
AN UNUSUAL EDUCATION 21

Chapter Three
AN EXCITING TIME TO BE ALIVE 33

Chapter Four
WORK WITH CHARLES BABBAGE 46

Chapter Five
THE FIRST PROGRAMMER 61

Chapter Six
ADA LOVELACE'S LEGACY 74

TIMELINE 88
GLOSSARY 92
FOR MORE INFORMATION 95
FOR FURTHER READING 99
BIBLIOGRAPHY 104
INDEX 108

INTRODUCTION

A tech pioneer is someone who pushes the limits of technology. That person can be someone who creates the gasoline engine or a brand new type of telescope. It can be someone who revolutionizes the mobile phone. All that is required is a vision and the persistence necessary to bring that vision to life. Sometimes the tech pioneer can foresee the future applications of the work. Often he or she cannot see much past solving a vexing problem in the present. What all tech pioneers have in common is a vision for a new way to do something or a way to do something that has never before been possible.

The first person to use fire to cook food was a tech pioneer. So were the first people to use the wheel, the lever, and a piece of rock or charred wood to write or draw. They were tech pioneers because they took the existing technology—which may have been very low-tech in the very earliest cases—and brought it to a new level. In so

Ada Lovelace was the daughter of Lord and Lady Byron. She was also one of the first female tech pioneers.

doing, they opened the door for newer uses and types of technology.

Today we enjoy the results of the work of generations of tech pioneers who came before us. We ride in cars, fly in airplanes, and watch on television as shuttles head into space to rendezvous with space stations. We use ultrasound for diagnostic purposes and sonar to track our movement underwater. We use radar to keep track of objects moving through the air and radar guns to calculate the speed of cars in motion. Each of these technological innovations is possible because of the vision of a tech pioneer.

The tech pioneers started with bicycles and engines that evolved into cars. They started with glider wings strapped onto their bodies that evolved into airplanes. They started with rockets with liquid propellants that evolved into space shuttles. They started with radios and transistors that evolved into televisions. Each of the technologies we enjoy today started with the vision of a tech pioneer and was taken to new levels by the tech pioneers who took what they had and moved that technology to the next level.

Ada Lovelace was a tech pioneer. She was also a woman who was involved in technical innovation far before the time when it was common for women to be involved in these types of endeavors. She was instrumental in bringing the first generation of mechanical computers to life. Her understanding of not just the workings of the machines but also the potential for these machines helped to bring them to the attention of the world. Her first attempts at programming pushed the boundaries of what the mechanical computer might do to what the mechanical computer could do. In the process, she opened the door to the advanced computer technology we take for granted today.

The story of her growth from curious child to visionary woman is the story of a tech pioneer.

Chapter One

England in the Time of Ada Lovelace

Augusta Ada Byron was born on Sunday, December 10, 1815. She was the only child of Lord Byron and Anabella Milbanke. The two parents could not have been more different in their talents and worldviews. Lord Byron was a famous poet, noted for his wild lifestyle and romanticized view of the world. Anabella Milbanke was a highly educated woman who was strictly religious. She lived by a strong moral code. Byron described her as "the Princess of Parallelograms" because of her love of mathematics and logic. Their daughter would spend her life carving out her space between the two.

Lord Byron and Anabella Milbanke were married nearly a year at the time of Ada's birth. Byron wrote that the child that he called Ada was "the child of love—

though born in bitterness, and nurtured in convulsion." Although Lord and Lady Byron legally separated when Ada was only a month old, and Lord Byron left the country soon after, he maintained an active interest in Ada, often sending her things through an intermediary. It is said that his dying words expressed his regret that he would not live to see his daughter.

Ada grew up hearing her father disparaged at home and vilified in the press. The society she grew up in was not tolerant of promiscuous behavior, and Lord Byron was known for that and more. The only image of him in the house was hung facing the wall. It wasn't until Ada's twentieth birthday that her mother turned the picture around and she finally saw what her father looked like.

The fact that Lady Byron had obtained custody of Ada after her separation from Lord Byron was highly unusual for that time. The arrangement was a result of a mental evaluation into which Lady Byron had tricked Lord Byron. When it was determined that Lord Byron's dark moods and erratic behavior were truly a cause for concern, Lady Byron insisted that she be granted custody of her daughter.

With everything that had been written about him and all that he had done, Lord Byron was hardly in a position to argue the point. He signed the legal separation agreement, and Lady Byron took Ada to live with her parents. Concerned that Lady Byron would one day

ADA LOVELACE

Lord Byron was equally well-known for his poetry and his questionable behavior.

leave the country for good, Lord Byron insisted that Ada be made to stay in England. Lady Byron often visited other countries for health "cures," but she respected Lord Byron's wishes in this matter and left Ada behind in England whenever she was traveling.

For his part, Lord Byron did not enjoy the best of reputations. When Lady Byron left him to take Ada to live with her parents, public opinion was firmly on her side. Lord Byron was frequently in the press for his wild ways. Ultimately, he grew tired of his notoriety and left England in search of a clean slate and new challenges. Even after he left England, the rumors and innuendo continued. Because of this, Byron chose to stay abroad.

A Time of Arts and Innovation

Ada lived during a period of great change in Great Britain. Napoleon Bonaparte was defeated at Waterloo in the year of her birth. Queen Victoria took the throne when Ada Lovelace was in her early twenties. The Great Exhibition, at which exciting new technology of the time was displayed to the public, was held in London the year before she died.

The fine arts blossomed during Lovelace's lifetime. *Pride and Prejudice* by Jane Austen was published before her birth in 1812. Other works by Austen followed.

ADA LOVELACE

A WOMAN'S ROLE

In Ada Lovelace's time, women did not work outside the home. Women were also not educated to the same extent as men. Women were expected to be able to make polite conversation, to dance and to embroider, to play the piano, and to make a good appearance on the many social calls they made. If they were wealthy, they were expected to manage a household staff, although dealing with money was the job of the man of the house.

Wealthy women such as Ada were presented to society and were thereafter expected to attend balls and other society functions. The opera and social causes were also activities that women considered important. Once a woman had children, there would be a governess in addition to the other household servants. The children would be cared for by the governess and educated by the governess and tutors as needed. They would largely spend their time at home until they were old enough to leave for school (if they were boys) or get married (if they were girls).

The life of a female was very controlled, with little access to the ideas and opinions of others unless those ideas were expressed by tutors or others known to the family. After marriage, a woman had more opportunities to attend lectures or to be out in society, but it was considered improper for a woman to have an opinion, let alone her own theories about mathematics and machines. Ada Lovelace would grow up to have both, making her an attractive and alluring anachronism.

Frankenstein by Mary Shelley was published in 1818. The first mystery, *Murders in the Rue Morgue*, by Edgar Allan Poe and *A Christmas Carol* by Charles Dickens were published in 1842 and 1844, respectively. The Brontë sisters were writing during this time, too. *Jane Eyre* appeared in print in 1847. *Moby Dick* by Herman Melville was published in 1851.

The Romantic poets were at their peak during Lovelace's lifetime. Work by Samuel Taylor Coleridge, William Blake, John Keats, William Wordsworth, and Robert Burns was being published. Painters such as Thomas Gainsborough and John Constable were also producing works that are still in high regard.

Invention flourished as the pace of invention and an attitude that embraced innovation took hold. The Industrial Revolution, spurred by the introduction of the steam engine in the late eighteenth century, caused great changes in English society. It was now possible for someone who was not born to wealth to achieve it as a factory owner or other merchant. It was also possible to produce more than enough of a product. This allowed the surplus

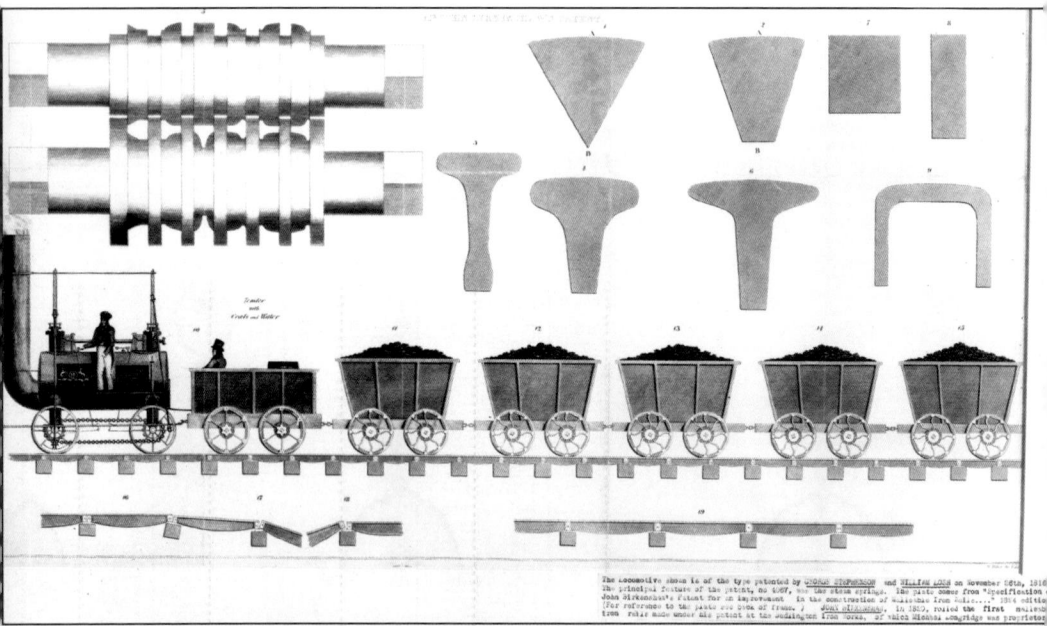

The introduction of the steam engine and working railroads brought about rapid change in British society.

to be sold in markets outside of the United Kingdom. As a result, an active interest in other countries was also a notable feature of the era.

In keeping with the spirit of discovery, the Rosetta Stone was deciphered in 1822. Many of the things we take for granted today were introduced during Lovelace's lifetime. Some of these are the stethoscope (1816), the combustion engine (1823), the steam locomotive (1824), and the first working refrigerator (1834). With so many processes that had been done by hand now being done by machine, attention was being paid to ways to speed up or automate the processes.

THE FIRST WORLD'S FAIR

By the time Queen Victoria had been on the throne for almost fifteen years, her husband, Prince Albert, became convinced the time was right for England to promote its products to the world. In both England and France, small exhibitions of manufactured goods had been held for many years.

These showcases were seen as a way to promote the country's goods and spur international trade. Prince Albert was certain that a large exhibition to

Victoria was crowned queen in 1837. Her reign was known as the Victorian era.

THE VICTORIAN PERIOD

The Victorian period in British history began when Victoria became queen in 1837 after the death of King William IV. It ended with her death in 1901. The Victorian period was a time when Britain grew in power. It expanded its reach into Africa, India, and other areas on the Asian continent. The claim could be truthfully made that the sun never set on British soil.

In Britain itself, there were some significant changes that took place. During the reign of Queen Victoria, the middle class began to grow. Until the Victorian era, the major factor in a person's life was the class into which he or she had been born. With the possibility of moving up in status came a new regard for the importance of doing things "right" and acting "properly." It also introduced some uncertainty into the status of any individual family. In the Victorian period, it was possible for a family to advance, at least a bit, through hard work and hard-won connections.

The Brontë sisters and Charles Dickens wrote during Queen Victoria's reign. In contrast to Austen's novels, where the right marriage was the key to economic security, the Brontës and Dickens wrote about characters that were striving to make a life for themselves that was not confined to their class at birth. Poets of the time included Robert Browning, John Donne, and Alfred Lord Tennyson.

> With its newfound power and influence came increased pride in all things British. The Great Exhibition was held in London as a way to garner more trading opportunities and showcase British goods from the Industrial Revolution to the world. The Crystal Palace, an elaborate building built of cast iron and plate glass, was the home of this exhibition.

show British goods could only lead to significant trading opportunities, especially since Parliament had adopted free trade to promote international sales of British goods.

The Great Exhibition Prince Albert envisioned would be the first world's fair. Also known as the Crystal Palace Exhibition or the Great Exhibition of the Works of Industry of All Nations, it brought international attention to the wide variety of goods that were available from British industry and set the standard for the world's fairs that quickly followed. The goal of this first world's fair, as well as of those that followed, was to celebrate the accomplishments of industry around the world. Each world's fair would highlight the work of the host nation, as well as the work of the nations that sent exhibits. For the first time ever, people in a variety of countries became aware of the work being done and the accomplishments being made in countries they had never visited.

Hosting the world's fair was an honor. As host, England wanted an exhibition hall that was special and notable. The Crystal Palace was the building erected to house the exhibits. It was made of cast iron and plate glass and designed by Sir Joseph Paxton after the nearly 250 designs submitted to a competition to select a design were rejected by the design committee. The Paxton design featured the most glass ever used in a building. It was as much an example of English ingenuity as were the goods housed within.

We know from correspondence of the time that Ada Lovelace, who was in her thirties by then, was an enthusiastic visitor to the Great Exhibition. It

fit with her interests, as well as her association with noted thinkers of the time in science and math.

Ada Lovelace was a remarkable woman for her time. Her education in advanced mathematics prepared her to

The Crystal Palace was designed by Joseph Paxton. It housed the Great Exhibition.

pursue her curiosity in areas that were not open to most other women. Her acquaintance with notable thinkers, including other women who were well educated in mathematics, gave her the unusual opportunity of being able to hear about the latest theories and investigations from those who were most familiar with the work. The result was that Lovelace was in the rare position of being able to put her informed and inquisitive mind to use pursuing her interests in science and the new technology at a time when great change was taking place. She was ideally situated to be a tech pioneer.

Chapter Two

An Unusual Education

Lady Byron, Ada Lovelace's mother, was highly educated for a woman of her time. She had received the equivalent of a Cambridge University education from her tutor, William Frend. That education included work in classical literature, philosophy, science, and math. Having seen firsthand the benefits of such an education, she was eager for her daughter to receive a comparable education. Lady Byron was also very concerned that without proper discipline, Ada would develop the dark moods and erratic behavior of her father, Lord Byron. Lady Byron attributed these moods to the fact that Lord Byron was a poet. To guarantee that Ada did not develop her father's "illness," Lady Byron insisted that Ada study mathematics from an early age.

ADA LOVELACE

Ada's mother insisted on a mathematical education for Ada as a way of ensuring she did not develop the character traits of her father, Lord Byron.

WHO WAS LORD BYRON?

George Gordon Noel Byron, the 6th Baron Byron, lived from 1788 to 1824. One of the most famous of the Romantic poets, he died in Missolonghi, Greece, while fighting with the Greeks for their independence.

Lord Byron was as noted for his dark moods and wild behavior as he was for his poetry. The heroes of his works—the Byronic heroes—were often moody, unrepentant sinners who didn't have much use for polite society and its rules. They were drawn to forbidden experiences and tended to act in ways that were harmful to themselves. He also wrote of unrequited love, in which the man was attracted to a lady who did not return the affection.

Much of the criticism of Lord Byron focused on his personal life. He was known for his wild love life and inappropriate behavior in public. He was also very handsome. British poet Samuel Taylor Coleridge wrote of him, he was "so beautiful a countenance. I scarcely ever say. ... his eyes the open portals of the sun—things of light, and for light." He had a number of close friends, and those who were loyal to him stayed loyal to the end.

Mary Shelley, author of *Frankenstein*, described Byron as "the fascinating—faulty—childish—philosophical being—daring the world—docile to a private circle—impetuous and indolent—gloomy and yet more gay than any other. ... [I become] reconciled (as I used to in his lifetime) to those waywardnesses which annoyed me when he was away, through the delightful and buoyant tone of his conversation and manners."

Some of Byron's most famous works are "She Walks in Beauty," "Childe Harold's Pilgrimage," and "Don Juan."

Ada's Formal Education

Ada's formal education began at the age of four. She was taught by a series of governesses. When there was no governess in place, Lady Byron would instruct her. The instruction took place from morning until evening. If Ada did as she was told, she would get a strip of paper to use for a reward. When she disappointed her mother, she would lose a strip. If she was completely disobedient and not inclined to study that day, Lady Byron would lock her in a closet until Ada was ready.

On Sundays, when Ada did not have formal instruction, her governess would supervise as Ada worked with blocks. This was in keeping with the education theories and program of Pestalozzi, the Swiss educator who was one of the first to approach instruction from a child's point of view. Even at a very young age, her governess noticed that Ada was excited to

An Unusual Education

Ada Byron, age four. Even at this tender age, the young girl was subjected to hours of instruction at the insistence of her mother.

work with the blocks in forming structures of her own, rather than assembling them as instructed or following someone else's plan. This is noteworthy because as an adult, Ada would often seek out three-dimensional models to assist her in her understanding of shapes and concepts.

Dr. Frend advised Lady Byron that it was unwise to put so much pressure on a four-year-old. Lady Byron was undeterred. She had a system in place, and she was determined to keep it in place. When Ada told her mother one day that she wished she could get to the end of arithmetic, Lady Byron was not pleased. To appease her mother, Ada wrote in her journal, "I was rather foolish in saying that I did not like arithmetic and to learn figures, when I did—I was not thinking quite what I was about. The sums can be done better, if I tried, than they are."

From his distance, Lord Byron was much more tolerant of Ada's interest in mathematics than Lady Byron was about any potential interest Ada might have in the arts. When told about her mathematical interests, he is believed to have said, "One poet in the family was enough."

When Ada was seven, she became very sick with an illness that affected her eyesight and gave her headaches. Doctors advised that her formal education should be stopped until she was feeling better. Lord Byron was very concerned when he heard this news. Even though he hadn't seen his daughter since her infancy, he had kept up with the progress of her life. For her part, Ada knew nothing about her father that came from direct experience, but she nonetheless felt a deep connection to him.

ADA'S FLYING MACHINE

In 1828, when she was thirteen, Ada decided to build a flying machine. This was before the publication of George Cayley's seminal work on aviation. It was also decades before Alphonse Penaud would experiment with twisted rubber to power a tiny propeller. Otto Lilienthal had not yet begun his gliding experiments in Germany. Octave Chanute had not undertaken his gliding experiments in the United States. Neither had Samuel P. Langley. The Wright brothers had not begun the experimentation with "wing warping" that would lead to their first successful flight at Kitty Hawk.

Ada had just returned from a fifteen-month tour of the European continent, where she had lived a life filled with adventure, lights, colors, and sounds that were new to her. Upon their return, her mother had left England for a "cure," and Ada was bored. She was intrigued by the story of Daedalus and his attempts to fly with wax and feather wings. What better thing to do than try to fly?

Ada set out to build a flying machine. She proceeded in her usual logical and thorough fashion. The first thing she needed was wings. She made a thorough investigation of the anatomy of birds to find the proportion of wing to body. She assessed the suitability of materials ranging from wire to paper. To record her findings, she wrote a book, *Flyology*, which included drawings of her designs.

When it seemed, correctly, that human-powered wings would not do, Ada began to investigate steam power. She decided she would put the apparatus inside a vessel that looked something like a Pegasus. The wings would be powered by the steam engine.

When her mother discovered that Ada was neglecting her studies to work on this project, she insisted Ada stop at once. Ada decided to put a wooden horse in the room and pretend she was flying on a real horse instead.

The next year, when Ada was eight, Lord Byron died in Greece. Ada cried when she heard the news, a reaction her mother didn't understand.

Ada's governess and confidant, Miss Stamp, left her position to marry when Ada turned thirteen in 1828. To take the place of Miss Stamp, Lady Byron set about finding suitable teachers for Ada. She was in the process of obtaining the cooperation of three friends for Ada's future educational pursuits when Ada caught the measles. This was even better for Lady Byron's plans, since Ada was confined to bed for nearly six months and Lady Byron could control her more easily. Miss Arabella Lawrence was hired to educate Ada during the time she was confined to bed. Most of Ada's education took place by correspondence, with visits every few weeks.

Lady Byron not only read Ada's letters to Miss Lawrence, but she also added her own comments. She also warned Miss Lawrence of Ada's tendency to be biting and rude, telling Miss Lawrence it was "very necessary for this habit to be checked, both as disagreeable and inconsistent with the feeling of respect."

Ada was miserable with this arrangement and tired of being stuck in bed. By the time they moved to a new estate in 1832 and Ada was able to be up and about, she was overweight and out of shape. She also was faced with a series of tutors for chemistry, Latin, shorthand, and music. She had no governess, but her mother had three friends keep a close watch on her when she was away. Ada hated this and referred to them as the three Furies, after the mythological goddesses of vengeance.

As she grew older, Ada also tried to reconcile her interests in science with the way she viewed the world. She was realizing that, to her, the world was not a black and white place. The things she could imagine could be brought about by science and math; she was sure of that. The fact that something came to her as an idea first and was then realized through facts and numbers did not diminish her excitement or her creativity. But in Ada's life, creativity and imagination were viewed as things to be avoided and squashed where possible. The quest to

Ada Lovelace

Lady Isabella Milbanke Byron, Ada's mother, viewed imagination as something to be quashed and avoided.

combine or reconcile the two different ways of thinking would occupy Ada into adulthood.

Ada and Lady Byron

Ada and her mother were both gifted mathematicians. They were also both very well educated for women of their time. That is where the similarities ended. As a result of her frightening and humiliating experiences with Lord Byron, Lady Byron saw the arts as a dangerous pathway to mental derangement and improper behavior. Ada did not view the arts in this way. She saw the arts as another side of mathematics, a side that helped her to see the possibilities of a technique, solution, or machine.

Lady Byron also had a very clear view of the dark side of Lord Byron's personality. Ada could not. All she knew of her father came through the lens of the experience of others. To her, he was as romantic a figure as one of the characters in his works. His death in a foreign country, helping fight for the cause of freedom, only added to his mystery. This differing view of her father did little to endear her to her mother.

Ada Lovelace was a well-rounded person despite the lopsided formal education she'd received. She was interested in the arts, and once she came of age she had ample opportunity to pursue those interests with visits to galleries and exhibitions. Her interests continued along the path she'd first pursued with the flying experiment. She tended to blend imagination with experimentation and deep reflection.

Ada tried to include her mother in her view of the world. She was desperate to bring the worlds of her parents together since she was the product of them both. She would later articulate the relationship of mathematical science and imagination in a letter to the mathematician Charles Babbage. Mathematical science showed what is, she said, but "imagination too shows what is, the is that is beyond the senses." By combining the two, she was recognizing, great breakthroughs could be made.

Ada shared this insight with her mother, telling her of the time she'd spent on mathematics and the ways in which her work inspired her imagination. She told her mother that although it seemed strange, she might soon be a poet. Ada meant this as a way to express her desire to use her intellect and imagination to spur her creativity, but this was about the last thing Lady Byron ever wanted to hear from her daughter. Her relationship with Ada would continue to be strained for the rest of Ada's life.

Chapter Three

An Exciting Time to Be Alive

Ada Lovelace was presented at court on May 10, 1833. Once she was out in society, her life opened up in pleasing ways. One way had to do with her social life. She was of an age where invitations to social functions brought her into contact with very influential and learned people. One such person was Charles Babbage.

Charles Babbage

Ada met Charles Babbage at a party on June 5, 1833. She was seventeen, and he was a forty-two-year-old widower. He was already well established and recognized as one of the foremost mathematicians of his time. He also had unusual views on politics, science, technology, and

Charles Babbage was recognized as one of the most important mathematicians of his time.

WHO WAS CHARLES BABBAGE?

Charles Babbage (1791–1871) was a noted mathematician and thinker. His work formed the basis of the first computer.

Babbage was passionate about math from an early age. He taught himself algebra and read so widely in mathematics that when he entered Trinity College, Cambridge, he was far ahead of his tutors. He worked to replace Newtonian mathematics with this new mathematics and cofounded the Analytical Society for this purpose in 1820.

Babbage worked as a mathematician, primarily in the then-new field of calculus of functions, while in his twenties. He was elected a Fellow of the Royal Society in 1816 and was a founding member of the British Astronomical Society in 1820.

In 1821, Babbage designed the difference engine. This machine was for a specific purpose—the preparation of tables for navigation—and could perform only one type of calculation without error—the calculation necessary to prepare the table. Babbage envisioned a machine that could perform any type of calculation. This would be the analytical engine.

Babbage was trying to build a machine that was ahead of the manufacturing abilities of his time. His theories were respected, however, and he received government funding to build prototypes of his machines. Babbage abandoned work on the difference engine to focus on the analytical engine. As a result, neither machine was completed during his lifetime.

A Swedish printer, George Schuetz, did construct a difference engine in 1854. It performed beautifully and was used by both the British and American governments for mathematical, astronomical, and actuarial tables.

Charles Babbage was a respected mathematician whose achievements would have been noted even if he had not designed the difference engine and the analytical engine. He worked tirelessly to promote funding for the sciences. He held the Lucasian chair of mathematics at Cambridge from 1828 until 1829. He also helped to establish the Association for the Advancement of Science and the Statistical Society.

mathematics. He had attended Cambridge, as had Ada's father, Lord Byron. To a young woman like Ada, who had never known her own free-spirited father, Charles Babbage must have been of instant interest on many levels.

Babbage invited Ada to see the difference engine within weeks of their first meeting. Ada immediately grasped the potential of such a machine for a variety of uses outside of simple, routine calculations. Lady Byron was concerned that Ada was looking at math as a way of understanding metaphysical concepts. She wanted Ada to study mathematics and mathematical concepts strictly for their own true purposes. She had her friend Dr. King keep in correspondence with Ada for the purpose of keeping her studies on track.

Ada was young and brilliant. She was learning to have confidence in herself and to ask questions that were mathematical in nature but not strictly about math. Dr. King was not able to supply satisfactory answers, so she went to her mother's old tutor, Dr. Frend, with questions about things like the nature of rainbows and the way they appeared in the sky. Since Dr. Frend was elderly by now, he referred Ada to Mary Somerville, a gifted mathematician in her own right. Not only was she an astronomer as well as a mathematician, she was also one of the first women to be inducted into the Royal Astronomical Society. Somerville would go on to be a great normalizing influence in Ada's life. Ada would often visit the Babbage home with members of the Somerville family.

Babbage's Soirees

Once Ada was included in Charles Babbage's social world, she often attended his Saturday night soirees. During these events, his home attracted such notable people as

Ada Lovelace

Ada Lovelace also had the opportunity to meet Charles Darwin, who would go on to write *On the Origin of Species* in 1859.

the Duke of Wellington, Charles Darwin, Michael Faraday, Andrew Crosse, Harriet Martineau, and Charles Dickens.

Each of these people had an area of specialization that was his or her passion. With Michael Faraday, it was the field of electromagnetism. In 1831, his work resulted in his discovery of electromagnetic induction, the principle behind the electric transformer and generator. His discoveries were essential to the use of electricity for a variety of purposes.

By 1838, Charles Darwin had completed his journey aboard the HMS *Beagle* and written the draft of his first thoughts on evolution. He did not make his thoughts widely known, preferring instead to gather more information and to write about his travels in a more general way. Surely he discussed some aspects of his work at the soirees.

Andrew Crosse was an early experimenter with electricity. He was known for doing experiments that resulted in bright flashes of light. People who lived near Crosse were not quite sure what to make of him and his electrical work.

In 1837, he wrote a paper for the London Electrical Society in which he presented an account of his work. The experiment he described involved running electricity through a solution of silicate of potash and hydrochloric acid with a chunk of oxide of iron. His goal was

WHAT IS THE DIFFERENCE ENGINE?

The difference engine is a mechanical calculator that was designed by Charles Babbage in the 1820s. It was designed to use moving parts to produce reliable answers to calculations involving polynomials. This type of calculation involves solving for x.

The difference engine was Babbage's answer to the problem of reliable tables for use by navigators, who charted the course for vessels crossing the ocean. These men put their lives, and the lives of others, on the line based upon the information contained in these logarithmic tables. When the information in the tables was incorrect, as it often was, it made it impossible to navigate reliably. Babbage reasoned that if a machine did the calculations and the tables were produced in the process, the information would be uniform and correct.

The difference engine was not as sophisticated as the computers of today, although it was more sophisticated than a simple adding machine. It could be set up to solve one operation and was designed to solve a series of problems on a number of variables. It also featured storage to keep interim answers. The machine used a series of cogged wheels for its calculations. When it reached ten, it would move the next wheel into position to carry the digit.

The difference engine earned its name because it calculated the value of a polynomial using simple addition

An Exciting Time to Be Alive

alone through a method known as the method of finite difference. This method made it possible to solve for the answer without using multiplication or division. There were seven registers in Babbage's difference engine. With the use of these registers, thirty-one-digit values could be computed for polynomials with terms up to x7.

Babbage received government funding for his difference machine, but the funding was not steady, and the machine was never actually built. Had it been built, it would have been as large as a room.

to cause the growth of artificial crystals of silica. Instead, on the fourteenth day of the experiment he noticed some white specks that ultimately grew into creatures having between six to eight legs.

Crosse expected an outcry from the scientific community, and that's precisely what he got. Since he could not explain his discovery, he could only give the precise steps he took to arrive at the point where the creatures, acari, appeared. It was finally decided that the creatures were mites that had hatched from eggs that were in the mixture.

The Duke of Wellington was responsible for French leader Napoleon's defeat at Waterloo in 1815.

In 1828, he accepted the post of prime minister. He was known as the Iron Duke because he was very unpopular due to his stance against many parliamentary reforms. Between 1830 and 1834, he was not part of the government. When he returned to government service in 1834, it was as foreign minister until his retirement in 1846. Here was a man who would have most certainly piqued the curiosity and admiration of Ada Lovelace.

Charles Dickens was already a noted author when he met Ada Lovelace. The two had a relationship that was close enough that he agreed to read a death scene from one of his novels to her as she lay dying.

Novelist Charles Dickens was one of Ada Lovelace's personal friends.

William King, Earl of Lovelace

On July 8, 1935, Ada married William King, whom she had met a short time before. He was ten years older than Ada and was aware that Ada had fallen in love with one of her tutors when she was younger. Ada's behavior at the time was not considered acceptable and her mother's friends, the Furies, advised that Ada should consider herself lucky to have William King as a husband. Ada understood this, and in a letter to her future husband, she explained that she would make a good wife in return for his favor of overlooking her indiscretion, but that she did not expect to hear about it in the future. With that statement, she made it clear that she was aware of her good fortune but would not accept having it held over her head for a lifetime.

By 1838, William King had been made an earl. This made Ada a countess and meant that they were quite wealthy and influential. Together they had three children: Byron, born in 1836; Anne, born in 1837; and Ralph, born in 1839. From time to time, Ada would mention the difficulties of managing a household with three young children while also pursuing her interests in math. Many of her letters from her mother during this time contain criticism of her parenting. Later letters between Ada and her children reveal that she had a warm relationship with the three of them.

Ada Lovelace

William King, Earl of Lovelace, became Ada's husband on July 3, 1935.

44

Her Role in Society

Ada Lovelace enjoyed the company of the aforementioned noted people of her time and many more. She was a well-educated woman who took growing confidence in her intellectual abilities. She viewed mathematics and imagination not as opposing forces but as forces that inspired one another and led to greater creativity and insights as a result. Her conversations with noted thinkers would only have spurred her to consider new ideas and new facets of ideas she already had in mind.

As the Industrial Revolution (circa 1760–1840) hit its stride and the Great Exhibition was in preparation, all things must have seemed possible. A building of glass was under construction. A machine designed to "think" was in the works. The free exchange of ideas was taking place at soirees and events throughout London. Ada would have been part of many of these events and exchanged ideas with many of these people. It must have been an exciting time to be alive.

Chapter Four

Work with Charles Babbage

In the 1800s, the French government set out to promote the extension of the decimal system by publishing complex logarithmic and trigonometric tables. This would both reinforce the use of the decimal system and make ocean navigation more reliable. The English government set out to accomplish a similar goal so that it could compete with France's ability to conduct trade more efficiently. It quickly became clear that human error and time were the two main impediments to the successful completion of this goal.

With scores of people working on the tables by hand, there were hundreds of opportunities for errors. Even the same table, calculated correctly, was subject to error when it was set into type or copied over by hand. Time was the other problem. No matter how quickly

Work with Charles Babbage

The difference engine could solve one problem using a series of dials.

these men worked, it was tedious and laborious work that necessitated care. It was going to take a while to produce one copy of the desired table, let alone multiple copies.

To Charles Babbage, it was clear that a machine could do the work without error and in a fraction of the time. The machine in question could be set to do just that one calculation in the most efficient way. Once the results of a few calculations were checked for accuracy, the machine could produce the tables without errors, in record time.

The machine that Babbage designed for this purpose was the difference engine. It was called that because it took the series of first and second differences from a polynomial expression to calculate the answer for any polynomial expression of the same type.

The difference engine would perform its calculation using a series of dials. Before Babbage could complete the prototype of his machine, he had an idea for a superior machine. The analytical engine would use punch cards to enable it to perform calculations for a variety of algebraic expressions, not just one.

Italian mathematician Luigi Menabrea wrote a paper describing the difference between the two machines. His was then the only paper on the topic. It was based upon his discussions with Charles Babbage and was written in French. Menabrea wrote:

WORK WITH CHARLES BABBAGE

Italian mathematician Luigi Federico Menabrea wrote the first complete paper on Babbage's work with the difference engine and the analytical engine.

"Such is the nature of the first machine [the difference engine] which Mr. Babbage conceived. We see that its use is confined to cases where the numbers required are such as can be obtained by means of simple additions or subtractions; that the machine is, so to speak, merely the expression of one particular theorem of analysis; and that, in short, its operation cannot be extended so as to embrace the solution of an infinity of other questions included within the domain of mathematical analysis. It was while contemplating the vast field which yet remained to be traversed, that Mr. Babbage, renouncing his original essays, conceived the plan of another system of mechanism whose operations would themselves possess all the generality of algebraical notation, and which, on this account, he denominates the Analytical Engine."

WHAT IS THE ANALYTICAL ENGINE?

The analytical engine was Charles Babbage's design for a calculator that could perform more than one function. Unlike his difference engine, a machine that would perform one type of calculation over and over again, the analytical engine would be able to perform a variety of operations accurately and consistently.

If the difference engine could be thought of as an adding machine, the analytical engine could be viewed as

Work with Charles Babbage

a programmable calculator. It would be able to produce more than tables of numbers for navigation or statistics, the goal for the difference engine.

The analytical engine would not only step beyond relieving men from the tedium of doing the same series of calculations over and over again, but it would also give them the ability to automate a wider range of operations that varied with a task.

The analytical engine would have a "store" for the variables and a "mill" that performed the operations. The data and other information needed by the engine would be supplied on punch cards. One set would be the "operation cards" and the other the "variable cards." By feeding the correct series of cards into the machine, any operation could be performed. The cards would essentially transform the machine into one that performed a specific function. Once the operation cards were created, they could be saved and used again to perform the same type of operation. This would ensure that the results were error-free.

Babbage envisioned his difference and analytical engines as machines to perform mathematical calculations. Ada Lovelace saw the analytical engine as a machine that could do more than crunch numbers. From the start, she recognized its potential for a wider range of applications. Her most important work would be in explaining the analytical engine and its possibilities to the world.

Babbage's analytical engine would use punch cards. These would make it possible to perform a variety of calculations with one machine.

In the paper Menabrea wrote after his discussions with Babbage, "Sketch of the Analytical Engine Invented by Charles Babbage," Menabrea went on to describe the workings of the analytical engine as described to him by Charles Babbage. Ada Lovelace had been suggesting to

Babbage that she might work with him for many years by the time this paper was published in 1842. It provided the perfect opportunity for Lovelace because it was decided that she would not only translate the paper but include her own notes on the paper as well.

The Work of a Lifetime

Ada Lovelace is best known for her work with Charles Babbage. While Menabrea did a masterful job of explaining the workings of the analytical engine, it was Lovelace who gave life to the possibilities of the machine in her notes. As had been the case with the difference engine several years before, Lovelace grasped at once the implications and possibilities of a machine that would use punch cards of two types—operation cards and value cards—to perform calculations for a variety of problems. She laid out her thinking in a series of seven notes.

Note A

In her first note, Lovelace begins by highlighting the difference between the difference engine and the analytical engine. She writes of the difference engine, "It can therefore, tabulate accurately and to an unlimited extent, all series whose general term is comprised in the above formula; and it can also tabulate approximatively between intervals of greater or lesser extent, all other series which are capable of tabulation by the Method of Differences."

Of the analytical engine she wrote, "[It] is not merely adapted for tabulating the result of one particular function and of no other, but for developing and tabulating any function whatever. In fact the engine may be described as being the material expression of any indefinite function of any degree of generality and complexity."

The Jacquard loom was an amazing piece of technology of the time. By using an early type of punch card, Jacquard was able to automate his looms to produce designs that were identical in every way, every time the cards were used. This precision and consistency had a tremendous influence on Babbage in his vision for the analytical engine. Lovelace described the way in which the use of large pieces of stiff paper were used in the loom to allow only certain portions of the mechanism to be in action at any one time so as to create designs that were identical to one another from one run to the next. This same action came into play with the analytical engine.

After describing the way in which the punched cards would describe the operation to be calculated, she writes, "We may say most aptly, that the Analytical Engine weaves algebraical patterns just as the Jacquard-loom weaves flowers and leaves." In this blend of the imaginative, poetic, and mathematical, Lovelace took her first

Work with Charles Babbage

Inspired by those used for Jacquard's automated looms, these punch cards were designed for Charles Babbage's analytical engine.

step toward bringing to the world the possibilities of this new machine.

Note B

In this section of her notes, Lovelace describes the storehouse—an early vision of what we today refer to in computers as RAM, or random access memory. Rather than describe it in vague terms that would not resonate with her readers, she described it in human terms,

WHAT IS A PUNCH CARD?

A punch card is a method for giving information or instructions to a computer. A punch card is also a means for storing data or entering values for use in a calculation.

In the early days of computing, punch cards were run through a reader at the start of any job a computer was to do. These cards were prepared on a special machine that punched holes in the cards in specific places to give instructions to a computer. When the cards were run through, the computer had what it needed to run the program and complete the instructions. Once a set of cards was created for a specific operation, those cards could be run through the computer each time that type of operation was needed.

The punch cards were rudimentary programs. They did not incorporate logic or decision rules, but they did step the machine through the process required to achieve an answer. Charles Babbage envisioned the use of punch cards for his analytical engine in the 1830s.

Herman Hollerith used punch cards in his electronic tabulator to prepare the results of the 1880 census. He entered a contest in which the one to tabulate the results most quickly would receive the contract for the 1890 census. The other two competitors took 144.5 hours and 100.5 hours. Hollerith took 5.5 hours. He won the contract and his machines with punch cards were used until the 1950s, when computers were used instead.

Hollerith had proven that punch cards could be used for the purpose of data tabulation. They were used as an input method on the first computers, too. A dedicated machine was used to prepare the cards. The cards were then put into a feeder that allowed the computer to read and interpret each card in turn.

"The reader may picture to himself a pile of rather large Draughtsmen heaped perpendicularly one above another to a considerable height, each counter having the digits from 0 to 9 inscribed on its edge at equal intervals; and if he then conceives that the counters do not actually lie one upon another so as to be in contact, but are fixed at small intervals of vertical distance on a common axis which passes perpendicularly through their centers, and around which each disc can revolve horizontally so that any required digit amongst those inscribed on its margin can be brought into view, he will have a good idea of one of these columns."

Even today, technical aspects of a computer or computer programs are often described in terms that do nothing for the reader's understanding. By taking what was then an entirely new concept and bringing it to the reader in terms that were applicable to the things they understood, Lovelace broke new ground and did so in a way that brought greater understanding to the general population.

Note C

The workings of the Jacquard loom cards are briefly discussed here. Lovelace notes that, "The mode of application of the cards, as hitherto used in the art of weaving, was not found, however, to be sufficiently powerful for all the simplifications which it was desirable to attain in such varied and complicated processes as those required in order to fulfill the purposes of an Analytical Engine."

In the days before the invention of the keyboard or touch screen, the only way to communicate with the processor of the computer was through these punch cards. The cards used by Jacquard for his designs were adequate to his purposes, but, as Lovelace explains, they were not up to the task of communicating the operations and information required by complicated mathematical equations.

Notes D and E

The use and treatment of variables in calculations using the analytical engine are described here. In these expla-

Work with Charles Babbage

The Jacquard loom used punch cards to create the same pattern over and over again.

nations, Lovelace is laying out the underlying operations of any computer system. The variables are named and can have any values. Some are inputs to the calculation; some are calculated along the way as interim steps to be used in additional calculations. The proper treatment of these variables is essential to the successful completion of an operation.

The use of cards for the calculations is also touched upon. The calculations are set. The way we arrive at miles per gallon does not vary, for instance. Neither does the way we calculate profit or loss for a corporation. The exact items and amounts may vary by company, but the formula is unvarying. Only by breaking the process to be followed from the values to be used can the potential of a computer be fully realized.

Ada Lovelace was the person who brought this idea to life in her notes. Without her explanation and examples, Babbage would not have been able to excite the imaginations of those who followed.

Chapter Five

The First Programmer

Ada Lovelace is often called the first programmer. Some argue that she was merely describing what Charles Babbage had described to her. Because of that, they claim that she was not the first programmer and that that honor should go to Charles Babbage.

Others argue that without Jacquard and his loom, there would have been no punch cards. Without the punch cards, there would have been no way to record the operations or the variables. Without Jacquard there would have been no programs. These people argue that the first programmer was Jacquard.

Still others argue that Charles Babbage described, in general terms, what he had planned, but that even he failed to grasp the full implications of the analytical engine. They

Ada Lovelace

J. M. Jacquard was the first to use punch cards to automate his weaving process, paving the way for Babbage's engines.

claim that he was looking at it, even at its best, as little more than a glorified calculator. They argue that Ada Lovelace was the first programmer because she was the first to grasp the full potential of the analytical engine.

Lovelace understood that this machine and ones like it would not only calculate a variety of expressions, but those results could then be used in a variety of ways to take the numeric results and turn them into useful information. Because of this, they claim, Ada Lovelace was the first programmer. The greatest support for this view lies in her Notes F and G to the Menabrea "Sketch of the Analytical Engine."

Note F

Lovelace's view of the process used with Jacquard's cards provides the reader with the first insight into Lovelace as a programmer. She is not content to simply get the desired result. She is interested in the efficiencies that can be gained by looking at the total process and breaking it into algorithms that can be written as programs and perfected.

For instance, she notes the existence of "a beautiful woven portrait of Jacquard, in the fabrication of which 24,000 cards were required." Lovelace explains that this number of cards would not be required, as explained by Menabrea, and also by herself in Note C, if cycles within the process were noted and accounted for.

Article XXIX.

Sketch of the Analytical Engine invented by Charles Babbage
Esq. By L. F. Menabrea, *of Turin, Officer of the Military Engineers.*

[From the *Bibliothèque Universelle de Genève*, No. 82. October 1842.]

[BEFORE submitting to our readers the translation of M. Menabrea's memoir 'On the Mathematical Principles of the Analytical Engine' invented by Mr. Babbage, we shall present to them a list of the printed papers connected with the subject, and also of those relating to the Difference Engine by which it was preceded.

For information on Mr. Babbage's "*Difference* Engine," which is but slightly alluded to by M. Menabrea, we refer the reader to the following sources:—

1. Letter to Sir Humphry Davy, Bart., P.R.S., on the Application of Machinery to Calculate and Print Mathematical Tables. By Charles Babbage, Esq., F.R.S. London, July 1822. Reprinted, with a Report of the Council of the Royal Society, by order of the House of Commons, May 1823.

2. On the Application of Machinery to the Calculation of Astronomical and Mathematical Tables. By Charles Babbage, Esq.—Memoirs of the Astronomical Society, vol. i. part 2. London, 1822.

3. Address to the Astronomical Society by Henry Thomas Colebrooke, Esq., F.R.S., President, on presenting the first Gold Medal of the Society to Charles Babbage, Esq., for the invention of the Calculating Engine.—Memoirs of the Astronomical Society. London, 1822.

4. On the Determination of the General Term of a New Class of Infinite Series. By Charles Babbage, Esq.—Transactions of the Cambridge Philosophical Society.

5. On Mr. Babbage's New Machine for Calculating and Printing Mathematical Tables.—Letter from Francis Baily, Esq., F.R.S., to M. Schumacher. No. 46, Astronomische Nachrichten. Reprinted in the Philosophical Magazine, May 1824.

6. On a Method of expressing by Signs the Action of Ma-

In this note she also explains that the analytical engine could perform calculations for problems that were yet unsolved. Here is the place where Lovelace, through the use of her imagination, love of technology, and deep understanding of mathematics, delves into the full potential of future computers.

She was absolutely correct in her conjecture that a computer could, "provided we know the series of operations to be gone through," provide a solution where none has been calculated before. This foresees a day when the computer could be used to solve problems of such complexity that they have gone unsolved for decades. This is absolutely one of the uses of supercomputers today.

It also reaches toward a time when computers could be used to formulate sophisticated models, using a number of variables, to arrive at a better understanding of such things as economic downturns, weather patterns, or global warming. None of these have definite answers. None of these has been definitively proven on a large scale, yet each of these types of models has been used to approximate reality and give the general public a better understanding of the underlying process.

Note G

This note is often referred to as the note that proves that Lovelace was the first programmer. In this note, she walks

IS IT AN ALGORITHM OR A PROGRAM?

An algorithm is a set of step-by-step instructions to solve a problem or complete a process. The steps can be those required to make a cake, build an automobile engine, or identify the highest number in a group of numbers. As long as the process can be broken down into individual steps, an algorithm can be used to instruct a person or machine.

An algorithm to find the highest number in a series of numbers might look like this:

1. If there are no numbers, then there is no highest number.
2. Assume the first number is the highest.
3. Compare it to the next number. If the next number is higher than your number, replace your current number with it and repeat step 3.
4. If there is no next number, your current number is the highest number.

A program would express this algorithm in a computer language known as C.

```c
int main()
{
    int array[50], size, i, largest;
    printf("\n Enter the size of the array: ");
    scanf("%d", &size);
    printf("\n Enter %d elements of the array: ", size);
    for (i = 0; i < size; i++)
        scanf("%d", &array[i]);
    largest = array[0];
    for (i = 1; i < size; i++)
    {
        if (largest < array[i])
            largest = array[i];
    }
    printf("\n largest element present in the given array is : %d", largest);
    return 0;
}
```

The difference between an algorithm and a program is that the first is expressed in terms that a human can understand while the second is expressed in terms that are for a computer. Different computers can interpret instructions in different computer languages, so the program may look different, but the algorithm is the same.

the reader through the calculation of a string of sophisticated expressions. Lovelace's mathematical genius and her deep understanding of the potential uses of the analytical engine are both evident here.

She begins by warning against "the possibility of exaggerated ideas that might arise as to the powers of the Analytical Engine. In considering any new subject, there is frequently a tendency, first, to overate what we find to be already interesting or remarkable; and, secondly, by a sort of natural reaction, to undervalue the true state of the case, when we do discover that our notions have surpassed

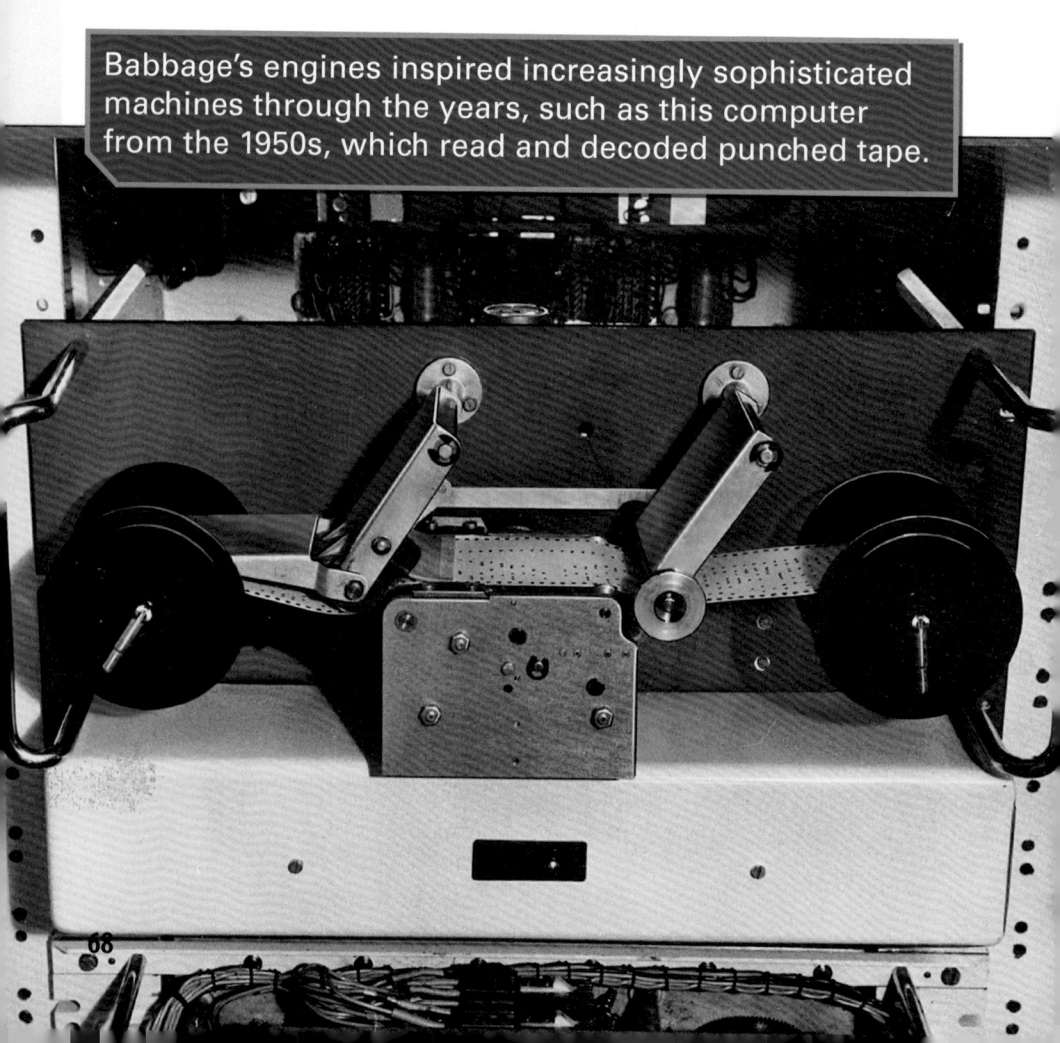

Babbage's engines inspired increasingly sophisticated machines through the years, such as this computer from the 1950s, which read and decoded punched tape.

those that were really tenable."

With this warning out of the way, she goes on to point out that "the Analytical Engine has no pretensions whatever to originate anything. It can do whatever we know how to order it to perform. It can follow analysis; but it has no power of anticipating any analytical relations or truths. Its province is to assist us in making available what we are already acquainted with."

Lovelace proceeds to walk the reader through a thorough and logical process for calculating the Bernoulli series using the analytical engine. It is likely that her most important contribution to the Notes was the fully realized set of the correct steps to be used in these calculations. Her insight into the process and her appreciation of the importance and possibility of recursive elements in the process, parts of the process that would be repeated, speak to her ability as a programmer and not simply a person who could describe the process in a general way.

WHAT IS A COMPUTER PROGRAMMER?

A computer programmer is the person who writes the code that instructs the computer hardware in what to do. The programmer may write a program that is as simple as the program required to calculate the grades for five people in one class with three tests each. It may be as

Continued from page 69

complicated as a program that calculates the grades for 500,000 students in kindergarten through grade twelve, attending 250 schools, and taking one or more of 1,000 possible classes with one or more of 3,000 different teachers.

Before the programmer can write the program, she must first have a thorough understanding of the process or problem. Anything she does not understand or misinterprets will be put into the program in a way that will include that error. That's why it's very important to test the program on data where the results are known. It's also important to have more than one set of data, supplied by more than one person or department, to test. Having more than one set of data and data that is supplied by more than one person will ensure that the programmer is writing code that is successful under a variety of circumstances.

Once the computer programmer uses a computer language to put the algorithm into a form the computer can understand, she must then test and find any bugs in the software. If the error is in a computation, that will usually show up quickly. If the error is in the logic, an error caused by a misunderstanding or misrepresentation of the process, that will take a bit longer to uncover.

When the computer programmer is done, there should be a program that works and gives the intended results each time it is run.

Lovelace's Vision

It is in Note G that the world first got a peek at what Ada saw as the full potential for the use of what would become known as the computer. She wrote of the use of the analytical engine, that the primary effect of the machine would be to calculate what we already knew how to calculate but,

> ... it is likely to exert an indirect and reciprocal influence on science itself in another manner. For, in so distributing the truths and the formulæ of analysis, that they may become most easily and rapidly amenable to the mechanical combinations of the engine, the relations and the nature of many subjects in that science are necessarily thrown into new lights, and more profoundly investigated. This is a decidedly indirect, and somewhat speculative, consequence of such an invention. It is however pretty evident, on general principles, that in devising for mathematical truths a new form in which to record and throw themselves out for actual use, views are likely to be induced, which should again react on the more theoretical phase of the subject. There are in all extensions of human power, or additions to human knowledge, various collateral influences, besides the main and primary object attached.

ADA LOVELACE

Charles Babbage read Lovelace's notes to the translation. It was at his urging that her notes were published along with the translation. At no time was Babbage unaware of what Lovelace had to say or the way in which she stated it. Because of that, we can only surmise that Babbage agreed with Lovelace's view of the capabilities

A diagram for the algorithm for computation of Bernoulli numbers using the analytical engine.

and potential uses of his analytical engine and the engines that would follow.

Ada Lovelace had no idea that one hundred years after her writing, we would be racing to be the first in space. She had no idea that one hundred fifty years later, we would be sequencing the human genome. She could not have known of quantum physics or nanotechnology, neither of which was envisioned in her lifetime, about the search for the Higgs boson, or about the use of computers in bioengineering. None of these ideas existed in her lifetime, but it is difficult to argue that these things would have been possible without the advances in science and technology brought about by the use of computers.

Chapter Six

Ada Lovelace's Legacy

Although Ada Lovelace is best known for her notes to the translation of Menabrea's essay, she had other accomplishments and interests as well. She enjoyed an active social life and attended many lectures, and she pursued her study of mathematics as an adult. She also took great pleasure, as seen in her correspondence, in her role as a mother. She took an interest in her children's activities and was happy to have them home as adults whenever possible.

Lady Byron often found reason to criticize Ada's parenting skills, but Ada seems to have been untouched by her mother's criticism. She did not share Lady Byron's views on education and did not try to contain any creativity or imagination in her children. Perhaps Ada remembered her own indiscretions and had a more tolerant point of view.

ADA LOVELACE'S LEGACY

Lady Byron, Ada's mother, continued to view Ada's outlook on life with disdain.

75

Ada Lovelace died of cancer on December 29, 1852. She was just thirty-seven years old. Ada and her husband had a private conversation during her illness. The content of the conversation is not known, but some have speculated that it concerned the circulating gossip that Ada had behaved inappropriately—possibly flirting—with another man. William King did not see or speak to her again. Charles Dickens came to read to her from one of his works while she was sick in bed. He was the last of her friends to see her before her death.

The thing that Lovelace is best known for was her unique ability to communicate about technology with an audience that understood nothing about that technology. Her deep interest in mathematics and science led her to seek the company of noted intellectuals of her time. Her interest in the foundations and fundamentals of mathematics led her to pursue her studies of math in its various forms throughout her life.

But Lovelace also had a wonderful imagination. She viewed mathematics and science as more than pure disciplines to be studied just for themselves. She viewed them as fields that held potential for a wide range of future applications. From the time she tried to build a flying machine as a girl until the time she wrote in Note G about the potential for new findings and expanded understanding in related areas in her late twenties, Ada Lovelace viewed science and math through what she termed a "poetic" understanding.

Ada Lovelace corresponded with many notable people of the day. This letter is to poet Ralph Waldo Emerson.

Lady Byron had no use for anything poetical. When Ada even suggested such a thing, Lady Byron would quickly turn a critical eye on anything else she could find to criticize, including Ada's parenting skills, to redirect the attention. She did not celebrate the genius that was Ada's—her ability to see technology and innovation for their full potential.

Despite Lady Byron's best efforts to the contrary, Ada's talent for viewing the world through both the lens of imagination and the lens of pure mathematical logic led to her unique ability to lead the world as a tech pioneer. Without this ability, she might have been able to describe the workings of Babbage's machines, but she would not have been able to fully envisage the potential

WHAT IS A COMPUTER LANGUAGE?

A computer language is used to communicate the set of instructions to a computer. Depending upon the level of the language, more or less is required of the person writing the program. At the lowest level of language, the programmer has to communicate specifically where values are to be stored. With higher-level languages, that is not necessary. The types of languages fall into several distinct groups.

Machine and assembly language are the lowest levels of computer language. Machine language communicates directly with the computer with strings of 0s and 1s. Programming in this language is tedious because everything is expressed by one of these two digits. Using machine language, the command to add two numbers might look like this "0110101111101000." Assembly language is slightly more sophisticated. It can be easily translated into machine language, but to the programmer it is "friendlier." Rather than a string of 0s and 1s, the command to add two numbers might be "add check, sum."

Algorithmic languages allow computer programmers to use standard formulas in their operations. These were the first high-level languages and are also able to use subprograms for commonly used operations. Some of these languages are FORTRAN, ALGOL, LISP, and C.

COBOL and SQL were the first business-oriented languages. COBOL made it possible to "speak" to the computer in "English." This meant that the instructions were closer to the way a programmer would think and express an idea. SQL made it possible to query a database and obtain the desired results.

BASIC, PASCAL, Logo, and HyperTalk were developed for use in learning to program. They are user friendly and relatively easy to learn. Object-oriented languages like C++, Ada, Java, and Visual Basic separate the data from the operations in a program. With the structure of the data hidden, the programmer can focus on the operation at hand.

uses for the analytical engine and types of technology that might come about after her lifetime.

While Manebrea's "Sketch of the Analytical Engine" was very well done, Lovelace's translation and her notes brought attention to the full range of possibilities of the machine. Without her notes, the magic of these machines would have been lost. They would not have been any less valuable to those performing routine calculations. They would not have been any less magical to those who saw them at work. But the idea that something wonderful was being introduced would easily have been overlooked. That would have been a tremendous loss because it is often those who see the introduction of new technology as a time when anything is possible who open their eyes to the full range of possibilities and become the tech pioneers we all respect and follow.

Anyone can make a circuit and light a bulb once the science is understood. It's up to someone open to the range of possibilities to see the potential for the scoreboards and Jumbotrons we all enjoy at sporting events. Anyone can ride on a road or observe a solar panel atop a house. It's up to a visionary to combine the two and create a version of the solar panel that will also work as a road.

Often the people who have the vision for the larger picture are not the people who make the initial discovery. After all, it took a tremendous amount of vision to make the discovery in the first place. Among the people who discovered the Higgs boson, the fundamental particle thought to be the source of all mass in the universe, are those who first envisioned the existence of the particle, then those who provided compelling proof for its existence, then those who thought of a means of proving its existence and worked to create the machine that would make it possible, and last but not least those who had the eureka moment of saying it had been found.

Communicating Technology to the Nontechnical

By being able to communicate both the exciting technical aspects of Babbage's work and its larger potential, Lovelace was among the first science writers. Her legacy is that she could communicate Babbage's work in a compelling manner, awakening the imagination of others in the process.

In recognition of her work as the first programmer, the Ada programming language was designed by a team within the Department of Defense. This language, worked on from 1977 to 1983, was used to replace the many languages being used. The idea was to have everyone on the same page, as the saying goes, so that maintaining the programs created would be a simpler task. It also meant that programmers from different areas would

WHAT IS A STEM CAREER?

A STEM career is a career in the field of science, technology, engineering, or mathematics. People who work in a lab or do scientific experimentation work in a STEM field. So do those who use science and mathematics to bring about technological innovation in fields like communication.

Science careers can range from careers in genetic research to the development of new pharmaceuticals. They can include careers as biologists studying animals in the field or chemists formulating solutions to the threat posed by environmental hazards. Scientists can work in private labs, government labs, or in the field.

Technology careers can include jobs for those who envision the next generation of mobile phones, Wi-Fi, or cars that drive themselves. The tech people are the ones who bring about ideas like drones and cars that parallel park without human intervention. They also are behind the newest security systems as well as the latest efforts to safeguard data transmitted over the Internet.

Engineers have STEM careers. Engineers may work in a variety of fields. These include civil engineers, who might work on the construction of dams and roadways; mechanical engineers, who might design the components for new machines; biomedical engineers, who might design artificial limbs and organs; or computer engineers, who might design computer components.

Careers in mathematics include work in quality control and statistical analysis, as well as academia. They can also involve careers in theoretical mathematics, in which new fields of math or new applications of mathematics are involved. Applied mathematicians bring mathematical solutions to existing problems. Mathematicians also work in epidemiology, forecasting the likely spread of a virus or other illness.

These careers have historically been considered fields for men. Women like Ada Lovelace have proved that women are more than capable of success in these fields.

be able to work together more easily.

The Ada program to produce the statement "Hello, world" would look like this:

```
with Ada.Text_IO; use Ada.Text_IO;
procedure Hello is
begin
   Put_Line ("Hello, world!");
end Hello;
```

The Ada programming language was designed both to create very large systems and to use English-like

Ada Lovelace

Ada Lovelace Day has been celebrated in mid-October each year since 2009. Lovelace is celebrated by many scientists, computer programmers, and mathematicians.

language. It is used less frequently today because there is a wide variety of available software out there. It is not the job any longer of government agencies to create their own languages.

Women Tech Pioneers

Ada Lovelace is also remarkable because she was a woman. Today, many take it for granted that a woman will have the same educational and career opportunities as a man. Although women are underrepresented in the sciences today, it is no longer novel that a woman would have a career in a STEM field. In Lovelace's time, this was certainly not the case. Because of this, she likely had an instant rapport with the few women, such as Mary Somerville, who were also active in the mathematics community.

Ada Lovelace was also young, very wealthy, and the daughter of a poet who was both famous and known for his bad behavior. It's certain that Lovelace was herself the source of conversation among those she met. For this variety of reasons, she was welcomed by a wide variety of the greatest minds of her time. She no doubt heard about their research and interests and saw the ways in which the work of each touched or overlapped on the work of another. These insights undoubtedly helped to fuel her imagination.

Ada Lovelace

Augusta Ada King, Countess of Lovelace, was not only the daughter of Lord Byron, she was also a tech pioneer.

It's hard to think of Lovelace as an adult, writing about the possible "various collateral influences, besides the main and primary object attached" to the analytical engine, without recalling the teenager who had ropes and pulleys attached in a room so that she could investigate the possibility of personal flight.

The same spirit that led to that wholehearted investigation into flight based upon a Greek myth seems to have survived unscathed into adulthood. The same lively imagination that envisioned herself with wings flapping could certainly have been excited about the vast potential in a machine that could calculate things we had never calculated and draw our attention to relationships between subjects and discoveries that had escaped our notice for generations.

Ada Lovelace's legacy was that she was able to carve a place for herself between the worlds of her parents. In so doing, she opened up the society of her time to the possibilities of a new technology.

Timeline

1788 Lord Byron is born.

1791 Charles Babbage is born.

1804 J. M. Jacquard invents cards for use in a loom.

1812 *Childe Harold's Pilgrimage,* by Byron, is published.

1815 Ada's parents marry on January 2.

1815 Augusta Ada Byron is born December 10.

1815 Napoleon is defeated at Waterloo.

1815 Steamboat service begins operating on the Thames.

1816 Ada's parents separate.

1816 Lord Byron leaves England.

1819 Ada's formal education begins.

1822 Ada's education is halted for a time due to illness.

Timeline

1824 Lord Byron dies.

1828 Ada works on a flying machine and writes *Flyology*.

1829 Ada gets the measles.

1833 Ada is presented at court.

1833 Ada meets Charles Babbage.

1833 Ada sees Babbage's difference engine prototype for the first time.

1834 Babbage gets the idea for the analytical engine.

1835 Ada and William King marry.

1836 Ada's son Byron is born.

1837 Ada's daughter, Anne Isabella, is born.

1837 Victoria is crowned queen.

1838 William and Ada become earl and countess of Lovelace.

1839 Ada's son Ralph Gordon is born.

1840 Lord Lovelace becomes lord lieutenant of Surrey.

1840 Babbage travels to Italy to discuss the analytical engine.

1840 Lovelace begins her study of mathematics with August de Morgan.

1842 L. F. Menabrea's "Sketch of the Analytical Engine" is published.

1843 Lovelace's translation and notes are published.

1851 The Great Exhibition is presented in London.

1852 Lovelace dies on November 27.

1871 Charles Babbage dies on October 14.

1890 Herman Hollerith uses punch cards for the U.S. Census.

Timeline

1979 The Department of Defense names its in-house programming language Ada.

1991 A working model of Babbage's difference engine is built by the London Science Museum.

2009 Ada Lovelace Day is launched. The commemoration is celebrated annually in mid-October.

2011 The first Ada Lovelace Day live event takes place.

Glossary

actuarial Measurement and statistical analysis of risk and uncertainty.

algorithm Step-by-step instructions for completing a task or calculation.

alluring Attracting attention in a way that draws someone close.

anachronism Someone or something that is out of step with the times.

assess To determine if something is suited for a specific purpose.

automate To create a process in which a machine carries out the task.

countenance Face or facial expression.

delve To dig deeply into a topic.

deranged Acting outside the normal or accepted standard of conduct.

Glossary

governess Woman employed by a wealthy family to educate the family's children.

ingenuity Using skill and inventiveness to solve problems.

innovation A new way of looking at something, for example, a new idea or product.

intervention Becoming involved so as to have an influence on people or events.

potential All that is possible for a person, place, or thing.

promiscuous Immoral, fast, sexually indiscriminate, unselective.

prototype A working model of a new product, designed to show that it can work.

rudimentary A basic version of something, often a first attempt.

striving Working hard to attain a goal.

surpass To do or attain more than has been done by something or someone else.

tolerant Putting up with something that is uncomfortable.

undeterred Not changing in the face of opposition or evidence to the contrary.

unrequited Not returned or fulfilled.

vexing Causing one to be worried, agitated, or annoyed.

Victorian era Period from 1837 to 1901, when Queen Victoria reigned and Britain expanded its power.

For More Information

American Association for the Advancement of Science (AAAS)
1200 New York Avenue, NW
Washington, DC 20001
(202) 326-6400
Website: http://www.aaas.org
The American Association for the Advancement of Science (AAAS) is an international organization created to advance science for the benefit of all people. Its site includes information about journals, careers, educational programs, and news.

Association for Women in Mathematics (AWM)
11240 Waples Mill Road, Suite 200
Fairfax, VA 22030
(703) 934-0163
Website: https://sites.google.com/site/awmmath/home
The Association for Women in Mathematics (AWM) was founded in 1971. Its mission is to encourage women and girls to study mathematics and to have active careers in mathematics. The website has a Girls in Math and Science page with lots of resources and info.

Canadian Mathematical Society
209 – 1725 St. Laurent Blvd.
Ottawa, ON K1G 3V4
Canada
(613) 733-2662
Website: http://cms.math.ca
The Canadian Mathematical Society is dedicated to the promotion of advancement in mathematics in Canada. It also sponsors events such as Connecting Women in Mathematics Across Canada and summer math camps. Information about Math Team Canada can be found on the website.

Canada Science and Technology Museum
1867 St. Laurent Blvd.
Ottawa, Ontario K1G 5A3
Canada
(613) 991-3044
Website: http://sciencetech.technomuses.ca
Canada Science and Technology Museum maintains a site that can be accessed in English or French. On the site, you'll find information about summer camps, professional days, the permanent collection, and visiting programs.

IEEE Women in Engineering
3 Park Avenue, 17th Floor
New York, NY 10016
(212) 419-7900
Website: http://www.ieee.org/membership_ser-
vices/membership/women/index.html?WT.mc_
id=WIE_nav1
IEEE Women in Engineering (WIE) is the largest international professional organization dedicated to promoting women engineers and scientists. They are also dedicated to inspiring girls around the world to follow their interests in engineering. The website has information about careers and educational opportunities.

Mathematical Association of America (MAA)
1529 18th Street, NW
Washington, DC 20036
(800) 741-9415
Website: http://www.maa.org
The Mathematical Association of America (MAA) has a range of programs. The organization also sponsors the American Mathematics Competitions (AMC).

Smithsonian National Air and Space Museum
Independence Avenue at 6th Street, SW
Washington, DC 20560
(202) 633-2214
Website: http://www.airandspace.si.edu
The National Air and Space Museum has thousands of objects on display. They also have an IMAX theater and planetarium. The website includes information about events, exhibitions, collections, research, and educational opportunities.

Websites

Because of the changing nature of Internet links, Rosen Publishing has developed an online list of websites related to the subject of this book. This site is updated regularly. Please use this link to access the list:

http://www.rosenlinks.com/TP/Love

For Further Reading

Adkins, Roy, and Lesley Adkins. *Jane Austen's England: Daily Life in the Georgian and Regency Periods*. New York, NY: Penguin Books, 2014.

Bentley, Peter. *Digitized: The Science of Computers and How It Shapes Our World*. Oxford, England: Oxford University Press, 2012.

Briggs, Jason R. *Python for Kids: A Playful Introduction to Programming*. San Francisco, CA: No Starch Press, 2013.

Cantor, G. N. *The Great Exhibition: A Documentary History*. London, England: Pickering & Chatto, 2013.

Dasgupta, Subrata. *It Began with Babbage: The Genesis of Computer Science*. Oxford, England: Oxford University Press, 2014.

DK Publishing. *History of the World in 1,000 Objects*. London, England: Dorling Kindersley Limited, 2014.

Essinger, James. *Ada's Algorithm: How Lord Byron's Daughter Ada Lovelace Launched the Digital Age.* Brooklyn, NY: Melville House, 2014.

Flanders, Judith. *The Victorian City: Everyday Life in Dickens' London.* New York, NY: Thomas Dunne Books, 2014.

Goldsmith, Mike, and Tom Jackson. *Computer.* New York, NY: DK Publishing, 2011.

Goodman, Ruth. *How to Be a Victorian: A Dawn-to-Dusk Guide to Victorian Life.* New York, NY: Liveright Publishing Corporation, 2014.

Isaacson, Walter. *The Innovators: How a Group of Hackers, Geniuses, and Geeks Created the Digital Revolution.* New York, NY: Simon & Schuster, 2014.

Johnson, Steven. *How We Got to Now: Six Innovations That Made the Modern World.* New York, NY: Riverhead Books, 2014.

Jones, Kevin. *Captain Max and the Armored Steam Balloon (Steampunk for Kids Book 1)*. Pele Products: Kindle, 2015.

Morrison, Philip, Emily Morrison, and Charles Babbage. *Charles Babbage on the Principles and Development of the Calculator and Other Seminal Writings*. New York, NY: Dover Publications, 2012.

Mullenbach, Cheryl. *The Industrial Revolution for Kids: The People and Technology That Changed the World, with 21 Activities*. Chicago, IL: Chicago Review Press, 2014.

Padua, Sydney. *The Thrilling Adventures of Lovelace and Babbage*. New York, NY: Pantheon Books, 2015.

Sande, Warren, and Carter Sande. *Hello World! Computer Programming for Kids and Other Beginners*. Shelter Island, NY: Manning, 2014.

Snyder, Laura J. *The Philosophical Breakfast Club:*

Four Remarkable Friends Who Transformed Science and Changed the World. New York, NY: Broadway Books, 2011.

Stanley, Diane, and Jessie Hartland. *Ada Lovelace*. New York, NY: Simon & Schuster Books for Young Readers, 2016.

Stratford, Jordan, and Kelly Murphy. *The Wollstonecraft Detective Agency Book 1: The Case of the Missing Moonstone*. New York, NY: Alfred A. Knopf, 2015.

Stratford, Jordan, and Kelly Murphy. *The Wollstonecraft Detective Agency Book 2: The Case of the Girl in Grey*. New York, NY: Alfred A. Knopf, 2016.

Swaby, Rachel. *Headstrong: 52 Women Who Changed Science—and the World*. New York, NY: Broadway Books, 2015.

Telles, Matthew A. *Beginning Programming*. Indianapolis, IN: Alpha, 2014.

VanderMeer, Jeff, and S. J. Chambers. *The Steampunk Bible: An Illustrated Guide to the World of Imaginary Airships, Corsets and Goggles, Mad Scientists, and Strange Literature.* New York, NY: Abrams Image, 2011.

Wallmark, Laurie, and April Chu. *Ada Byron Lovelace and the Thinking Machine.* Berkeley, CA: Creston Books, 2015.

Warrick, Patricia S. *Charles Babbage and the Countess.* Bloomington, IN: Authorhouse, 2007.

Woolley, Benjamin. *The Bride of Science: Romance, Reason, and Byron's Daughter.* London, England: Pan Books, 2015.

Bibliography

Babbage, Charles. *The Exposition of 1851: Or, Views of the Industry, the Science, and the Government, of England.* New York, NY: Cambridge University Press, 2013.

Babbage, Charles, and John Herschel. *Memoirs of the Analytical Society.* Cambridge, England: Cambridge University Press, 2013.

Byron, George G., and R. C. Dallas. *Correspondence of Lord Byron: With a Friend, Including Letters to His Mother.* Cambridge, England: Cambridge University Press, 2011.

Campbell-Kelly, Martin, William Aspray, Nathan Ensmenger, and Jeffrey R. Yost. *Computer: A History of the Information Machine.* New York, NY: Westview Press, 2013.

Dasgupta, Subrata. *It Began with Babbage: The Genesis of Computer Science.* Oxford, England: Oxford University Press, 2014.

Essinger, James. *Ada's Algorithm: How Lord Byron's*

Daughter Ada Lovelace Launched the Digital Age. Brooklyn, NY: Melville House, 2014.

Gibson, William, and Bruce Sterling. *The Difference Engine.* London, England: Gollancz, 2011.

Hellerstein, Erna O., Leslie P. Hume, and Karen M. Offen. *Victorian Women: A Documentary Account of Women's Lives in Nineteenth-Century England, France, and the United States.* Stanford, CA: Stanford University Press, 1981.

Higgs, Michelle. *A Visitor's Guide to Victorian England.* Barnsley, England: Pen & Sword, 2014.

Holyoke, Julie. *Digital Jacquard Design.* London, England: Bloomsbury Academic, 2013.

Jones, Capers. *The Technical and Social History of Software Engineering.* Boston, MA: Addison-Wesley, 2014.

Lovelace, Ada K., and Betty A. Toole. *Ada, the Enchantress of Numbers: Prophet of the Computer*

Age, a Pathway to the 21st Century. Mill Valley, CA: Strawberry Press, 1998.

Menabrea, L. F., and Ada Augusta, Countess of Lovelace. "Sketch of the Analytical Engine Invented by Charles Babbage." http://www.fourmilab.ch/babbage/sketch.html. Accessed May 11, 2015.

Morais, Betsy. "Ada Lovelace, the First Tech Visionary." *The New Yorker.* NewYorker.com, October 15, 2013. http://www.newyorker.com/tech/elements/ada-lovelace-the-first-tech-visionary. Accessed May 20, 2015.

O'Regan, Gerard. *Giants of Computing: A Compendium of Select, Pivotal Pioneers.* London, England: Springer, 2013.

Provenzo, Eugene F. *The Difference Engine: Computing, Knowledge, and the Transformation of Learning.* Lanham, MD: Rowman & Littlefield Publishers, 2012.

Regents of the University of Minnesota. "Who Was Charles Babbage?" http://www.cbi.umn.edu/about/babbage.html. Accessed May 11, 2015.

United States Census Bureau. "The Hollerith Machine." https://www.census.gov/history/www/innovations/technology/the_hollerith_tabulator.html. Accessed May 20, 2015.

Vickery, Amanda. *The Gentleman's Daughter: Women's Lives in Georgian England.* New Haven, CT: Yale University Press, 1998.

Index

A

Ada programming language, 81–85
Albert, Prince, 15, 17
algorithm, explanation of, 66–67
analytical engine, 35, 36, 48, 50–51, 53–55, 58–60, 61, 68–69, 73, 80
Austen, Jane, 11, 16

B

Babbage, Charles, 32, 33–37, 40–41, 48–53, 54, 56, 60, 61–62, 72, 81
Blake, William, 13
Brontë sisters, 13, 16
Browning, Robert, 16
Burns, Robert, 13
Byron, Lady (Anabella Milbanke), 8–11, 21, 24, 26, 28–31, 31–32, 37, 74, 78
Byron, Lord, 8–11, 21, 23–24, 26, 28, 31, 36

C

Christmas Carol, A, 13
Coleridge, Samuel Taylor, 13, 23
computer language, explanation of, 78–79
computer programmer, explanation of, 69–70
Constable, John, 13
Crosse, Andrew, 39, 41
Crystal Palace, 17, 18

D

Darwin, Charles, 39
Dickens, Charles, 13, 16, 39, 42, 76
difference engine, 35–36, 40–41, 48, 50, 51, 53–55
Donne, John, 16

INDEX

E
engineering careers, overview of, 82–83

F
Faraday, Michael, 39
flying machine, Ada's building of, 27–28
Flyology, 27
Frankenstein, 13, 23
Frend, William, 21, 26, 37

G
Gainsborough, Thomas, 13
Great Exhibition, 11, 17–19, 45

H
Hollerith, Herman, 56–57

I
Industrial Revolution, 13–14, 45

J
Jacquard loom, 54, 58, 61, 63
Jane Eyre, 13

K
Keats, John, 13
King, William, 43, 76

L
Lawrence, Arabella, 28, 29
Lovelace, Ada
  childhood and education, 8–11, 21–32
  death of, 76
  marriage and children, 43

M

Martineau, Harriet, 39
mathematics careers, overview of, 83
Melville, Herman, 13
Menabrea, Luigi, 48–50, 52, 53, 63, 74, 80
Moby Dick, 13
Murders in the Rue Morgue, 13

N

Note A, 53–55
Note B, 55–58
Note C, 58, 63
Notes D and E, 58–60
Note F, 63–64
Note G, 63, 65–69, 71, 76

P

Paxton, Sir Joseph, 18
Pestalozzi, 24
Poe, Edgar Allan, 13

Pride and Prejudice, 11
punch card, explanation of, 56–57

S

Schuetz, George, 36
science careers, overview of, 82
Shelley, Mary, 13, 23–24
"Sketch of the Analytical Engine," 52, 63, 80
Somerville, Mary, 37, 85
Stamp, Miss, 28
STEM careers, explanation of, 82–83

T

technology careers, overview of, 82
tech pioneer, explanation of, 4–6
Tennyson, Alfred Lord, 16

V

Victoria, Queen, 11, 15, 16

Victorian era, overview of, 16–17

W

Wellington, Duke of, 39, 41–42

women, role of, 12–13

Wordsworth, William, 13

About the Author

Gina Hagler is a science and technology writer for children and adults. She has written about STEM careers for girls. She blogs about science and technology at GinaHagler.com.

Photo Credits

Cover, p. 1 Print Collector/Hulton Archive/Getty Images; p. 5 Private Collection/Prismatic Pictures/Bridgeman Images; p. 10 Getty Images; pp. 14, 47, 52, 55 Science & Society Picture Library/Getty Images; pp. 15, 22 DEA Picture Library/Getty Images; pp. 18-19, 75 Hulton Archive/Getty Images; pp. 25, 38 Science Source; p. 30 Mansell/The LIFE Picture Collection/Getty Images; p. 34 Time Life Pictures/The LIFE Picture Collection/Getty Images; pp. 42, 68 Mondadori/Getty Images; p. 44 Eileen Tweedy/The Art Archive at Art Resource, NY; p. 49 DEA/V. Pirozzi/De Agostini/Getty Images; p. 59 Science Museum/SSPL/Getty Images; p. 62 DEA/G. Nimatallah/De Agostini/Getty Images; p. 64 Wikisource/Page:Scientific Memoirs, Vol. 3 (1843).djvu/676/CC BY-SA 3.0; pp. 72-73 Wikimedia Commons/File:Diagram for the computation of Bernoulli numbers.jpg; p. 77 Ralph Waldo Emerson Letters from Various Correspondents, ca. 1814-1882 (MS Am 1280, folder 1965), Houghton Library, Harvard University. File downloaded from Wikimedia Commons/File:Houghton MS Am 1280 (1965) - Lovelacejpg.jpg/PD-US; p. 84 Sarah Stierch/Wikimedia Commons/File: Ada Lovelace Day Celebration 2012 14.jpg/CC BY 3.0; p. 86 NYPL/Science Source/Getty Images; cover and interior pages VikaSuh/Shutterstock.com (light rays), evryka23/iStock/Thinkstock (light grid), Kotkoa/iStock/Thinkstock (circuit)
Designer: Brian Garvey; Editor: Christine Poolos; Photo Researcher: Nicole Baker